The Simple Little Book

on

English Tenses

Written by Tyler Garrison

Illustrated by Jesse Hickey

U0064314

1

The Simple Little Book on English Tenses

Author: Tyler Garrison
Illustrator: Jesse Hickey
Edition:1
Publisher: Stokes Learning and Literature
Publish date :2021.6
Website: www.et-ball.com

Contents

Introduction:

Question: What is the easiest way to teach English?

Answer: Make the lessons clear and simple.

How do I do this? Break down English into smaller subjects.

This book is on the subject of **tenses**.

The English Tense Ball teaches how to say the sentence patterns.

Pictures in the book help you imagine the moment so you can learn when to use each tense.

The method is original, engaging and fun! My students love it.

Remember! When you practice, *speak* every word out loud. After all, you are learning to *speak* English.

Let's get started!

-Tyler Garrison

Quick Lesson:

You will see the words *I/you/we/they/he/she/it/(Name)* often, but many sentences begin with more specific people or things.

If you say: *John and Jessica are coming.*

      The pronoun for *"John and Jessica"* is *'they'.*

If you say: *You and I like pizza.*

      The pronoun for *"You and I"* is *'we'.*

If you say: *The refrigerator is making noise.*

      The pronoun for *"refrigerator"* is *'it'.*

<u>More examples</u>	<u>Guess the pronoun</u>
our children-------------they	1. the trees--- _____
she and I----------------we	2. my family--- _____
Tim and George-------they	3. my family and I --- _____
my wife------------------she	4. Bill--- _____
John---------------------John	5. the park--- _____
the car-------------------it	6. the plants--- _____
the cars-----------------they	Answers are on the next page.

1. they 2. it 3. we 4. Bill (or) he 5. it 6. they

Simple Tenses

Present Simple

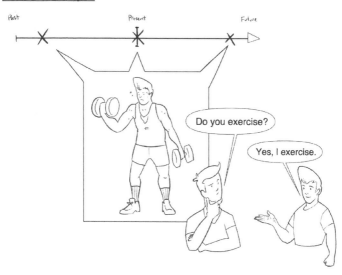

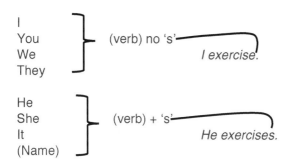

7

Make sentences: More verbs are on page 48-49.

Example: *What does he read? He reads adventure books.*

1. What _____ she play? _____ plays basketball.

2. Where _____ they eat? They _____ at the café.

3. Does Tom like pizza? Yes, Tom _____ pizza.

Present Simple is used for:

habits, routines, traditions

Where do you celebrate Christmas?
        I celebrate Christmas at my grandmother's house.

likes, wants, needs, beliefs, personal feelings

Do they like apples?
                Yes, they like apples.
(negative form) *No, they do not (don't) like apples.*

general truths, permanent actions, facts

Why does Tyler speak Spanish?
        Tyler speaks Spanish because he lived in Colombia.

Answers: 1. does/She 2. do/eat 3. likes

8

Words to use with Present Simple:

always-
> I **always** listen to music in the morning.

never-
> She **never** likes my jokes.

sometimes-
> He **sometimes** eats sushi.

usually-
> We **usually** watch the stars.

Make sentences:

Example: *She usually helps.*

1. Larry _____ rides his bike to work.

2. They _____ win.

3. I_____ work hard.

Past Simple

Verbs have a past tense form. You can add _'ed'_ to most verbs to make it past tense.

        jump -- jumped   kick -- kicked   wash -- washed

Do not add _'ed'_ to _irregular_ past tense verbs.

Here are some of the most common _irregular_ past tense verbs.

verb	irregular past tense verb
is	was/were
come	came
drink	drank
eat	ate
get	got
go	went
make	made
have	had
run	ran
see	saw
take	took
write	wrote

*More verbs are on page 48-49.

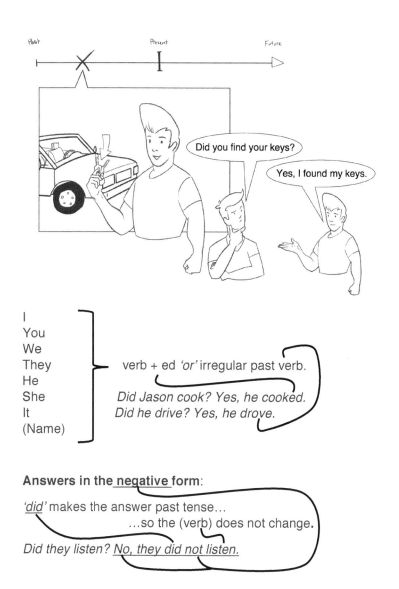

Past   Present   Future

Did you find your keys?

Yes, I found my keys.

I
You
We
They
He
She
It
(Name)

verb + ed *'or'* irregular past verb.

Did Jason cook? Yes, he cooked.
Did he drive? Yes, he drove.

Answers in the negative form:

'did' makes the answer past tense…

…so the (verb) does not change.

Did they listen? No, they did not listen.

Make sentences:

Example: *Where did you play?   I played at the park.*

1. What _____ she eat?   She _____ a hot dog.

2. Where _____ you go?   _____ went to the store.

3. _____ did he see? He _____ Carol.

Past Simple is used for:

past habits, hobbies or routines

Where did she study math?
        She studied math at Colorado State University.

actions already completed

Did you clean the house?
        Yes, I cleaned the house.
(neg)   *No, I did not (didn't) clean the house.*

Words to use with Past Simple:

yesterday-
> *I watched football **yesterday**.*

(number) seconds/ minutes/days/weeks/months/years ago-
> *Sally graduated **three years ago**.*

last week/month/year/day of the week -
> *We went to Spain **last Tuesday.***

in (year)-
> *We got married **in 1982**.*

Make sentences:

Example: *You played three weeks ago.*

1. We went to Spain _____.

2. Max and Sally walked to school _____.

3. I traveled _____.

*More verbs are on page 48-49.

Answers: 1. (any example word(s)) 2. (any example word(s)) 3. (any example word(s))

Future Simple

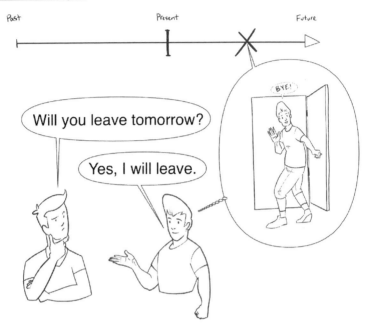

I		
You		
We		**will** (verb).
They		
He		*Will they leave? Yes, they **will** leave.*
She		
It		
(Name)		

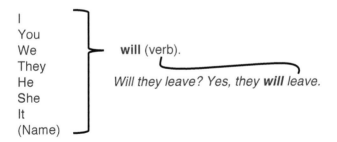

*A modal verb can replace *"will"* (the tense stays future simple.) More is on page 44.

Make sentences:

Example: *Who will we help? We will help Sue.*

1. Where _____ Carol go? Carol will _____ to France.

2. _____ will it rain? It _____ rain tomorrow.

3. _____ they work hard? Yes, _____ will work hard.

Future Simple is used for:

future predictions
Will they win the match?
        Yes, they will (they'll) win the match.
(neg)   *No, they will not (won't) win the match.*

future plans
When will you go with me?
        I will (I'll) go with you tomorrow night at 8:00.

future actions
Who will arrive on Wednesday?
        William will arrive on Wednesday.

Answers: 1. will/go 2. When/will 3. Will/they

15

Words to use with Future Simple:

tomorrow-
> *Sarah will race **tomorrow**.*

next week/month/year/day of the week -
> *They will meet with the director **next January**.*

soon -
> *I will finish my book **soon**.*

in (number) minutes/hours/days/weeks/months/years-
> *It will arrive **in 4 days**.*

someday-
> *I will travel to Africa **someday**.*

Make Sentences:

Example: *I will come in 20 minutes.*

1. Carol will race _____.

2. They will arrive _____.

3. I will see you _____.

*More verbs are on page 48-49.

"going to" can replace *"will"*

More details are on pages 46-47.

Continuous Tenses

Present Continuous

I **am** (verb) + ing.   *I **am** playing.*

You
We
They   **are** (verb) + ing.   *They **are** playing.*

He
She
It
(Name)   **is** (verb) + ing.   *Anne **is** playing.*

Make sentences:

Example: *Where are they playing? They are playing on the playground.*

1. *Is it working? Yes, it _____ working.*

2. *Why _____ they winning? _____ are winning because they are playing great.*

3. *What _____ she riding? She is _____ a bike.*

4. _____ *are* _____.

5. _____ *is* _____.

Present Continuous is used for:

actions currently happening
Where are we going?
    We are going to the park.

actions happening (but not at the moment)
Are you reading a novel?
    Yes, I am (I'm) reading a novel.
(neg)   *No, I am (I'm) not reading a novel.*

Answers: 1. is 2. are/They 3. is/riding 4. You, We, They...(verb) + ing 5. He, She, It, (Name)...(verb) + ing

18

Words to use with Present Continuous:

now-
> *The Broncos are playing **now**.*

Look-
> ***Look**, the bird is flying away.*

Listen-
> ***Listen**, the band is starting.*

Make sentences:

Example: *They are talking now.*

1. _____, *the birds are singing.*

2. _____, *a storm is coming.*

3. *The plane is landing* _____.

Past Continuous

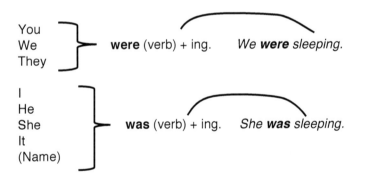

Make sentences:

Example: *Where were you walking? I was walking to school.*

1. *What was _____ eating? Jim _____ _____ pizza.*

2. *Why _____ they running. _____ were running because they wanted to exercise.*

3. *Was _____ raining? Yes, it _____ raining.*

Past Continuous is used for:

a past action that was in progress

Why were you laughing?
    I was laughing because the girl was funny.

telling a story *with* **Past Simple**

I was driving, and I saw John.

Words to use with Past Continuous:

at (time) -
> *You were sleeping **at 2:00 pm**.*

last week/month/year/day of the week -
> *I was traveling **last year**.*

yesterday -
> *They were working **yesterday**.*

while-
> *She was sleeping **while** he was driving.*

Make sentences:

Example: *I was studying last week.*

1. Jim was riding his bike _____ .

2. She was talking _____ I was sleeping.

3. They were traveling _____ _____ .

Future Continuous

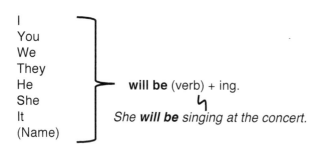

I
You
We
They
He
She
It
(Name)

will be (verb) + ing.

*She **will be** singing at the concert.*

*A modal verb can replace *"will"* (makes the tense Future Continuous or Present Continuous.)

More is on page 44.

Make sentences:

Example: *Where will he be working? He will be working in the office.*

1. Where will Jim _____ driving tomorrow? He _____ _____ driving to Los Angeles tomorrow.

2. Will they _____ talking at the party? No, _____ won't _____ talking at the party.

3. Why _____ he _____ working? He will be working _____ he needs extra money.

Future Continuous is used for:

planned future actions that will be in progress during a specific future moment in time

Where will you be eating tomorrow at noon?
        I will be eating in the park tomorrow at   noon.

with *(when)* **Present Simple**

*She will be speaking when **we leave**.*

Words to use with Future Continuous:

while-
> *She will be performing **while** we eat.*

during-
> *They will be talking **during** the movie.*

when (person) arrives/leaves-
> *You will be crossing the Pacific Ocean **when your baby arrives.***

Make sentences:

Example: *I will be working during the party.*

1. Jim will be singing _____ we dance.

2. I will be racing _____ they arrive.

3. He will be sleeping _____ the flight.

Perfect Tenses

Perfect tenses use Verbs in the past participle form (pp verbs).

verb	past participle (pp verb)
be	been
do	done
drink	drunk
eat	eaten
give	given
go	gone
have	had
know	known
make	made
see	seen
write	written
take	taken

*More pp verbs are on page 48-49.

Many students can *guess* the pp verb after learning the verb. Try it. You might be surprised!

Present Perfect

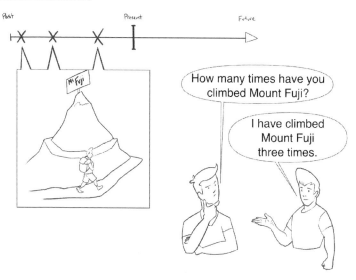

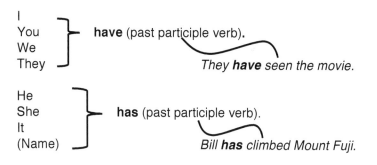

Make sentences:

Example: *Have they eaten? Yes, they have eaten.*

*1. Where have you traveled? I _____ _____ around
the world.*

*2. Have you _____ Titanic? Yes, _____ have seen
Titanic.*

*3. _____ he been to Spain? No, _____ hasn't _____
to Spain.*

Present Perfect (1) is used for:

past action completed at least once at an unknown time

Have you seen the ocean?
          Yes, I have seen the ocean.
(neg)   *No, I have not (haven't) seen the ocean.*

actions that are expected to be completed

Has he paid his bills this month?
          Yes, he has paid his bills.
(neg)   *No, he hasn't paid his bills.*

Answers: 1. have traveled 2. seen/I 3. Has/he...been

Words to use with Present Perfect (1):

ever-
> *Have you **ever** eaten tofu?*

since (day/month/year)-
> *I haven't seen a movie **since January**.*

the first time-
> *This is **the first time** she has written a book.*

never-
> *I have **never** seen an elephant.*

Make sentences:

Example: *They have never eaten Indian food.*

1. This is _____ _____ _____ Jim has run a mile.

2. I haven't seen Heather _____ 1991.

3. Has he _____ dressed up for Halloween?

Present Perfect (2)

Present Perfect (2) is used for:

actions performed in the very near past

Has the train arrived?
Yes, it has arrived.
(neg) *No, it has not (hasn't) arrived.*

Words to use with Present Perfect (2):

finally- *I have **finally** finished my book.*
*I have **finally** found The Grand Canyon.*

Make sentences:

1. We have _____ seen the Mona Lisa!

Past Perfect

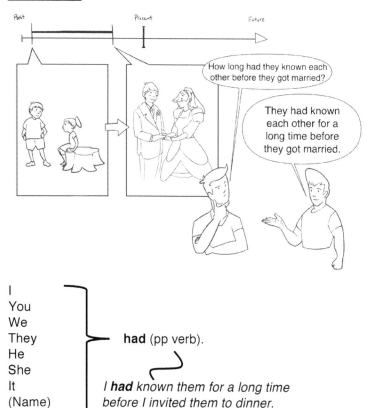

I
You
We
They   } **had** (pp verb).
He
She
It
(Name)

*I **had** known them for a long time
before I invited them to dinner.*

Make sentences:

Example: *Where had they been? They had been at the restaurant.*

*1. What _____ you eaten? I had _____ old sushi .
That's why I was sick.*

Answer: had/eaten

Past Perfect is used for:

sentences *with* **Past Simple** to refer to actions completed before a specific action in the past

Had you heard the band before you saw them play?
Yes, I had heard the band before I saw them play.
(neg) *No, I had not (hadn't) heard the band before I saw them play.*

Words to use with Past Perfect:

when –
They had known each other for 20 years **when** *they got married.*

already –
He had **already** *eaten dinner when I arrived.*

before-
We had eaten **before** *they served dinner.*

Make sentences:

Example: *We had ridden our bikes a long time when we found the store.*

1. *Jim had _____ made dinner when Melissa called.*

2. *I arrived _____ they decided to order pizza.*

3. *We had seen the movie Home Alone 12 times _____ Sue invited us to see it with her.*

Answers: 1. already 2. before 3. when

32

Future Perfect

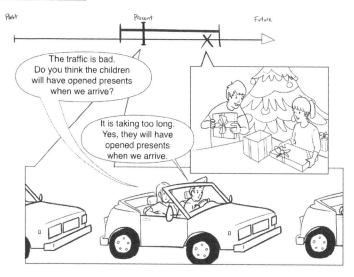

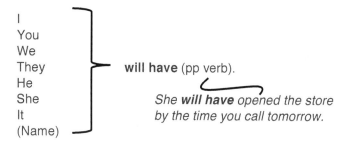

will have (pp verb).

She will have opened the store by the time you call tomorrow.

*A modal verb can replace *"will"* (makes the tense present perfect continuous.)   More is on page 45.

Future Perfect is used for:

future actions that will be completed before a specific future action

Will you have eaten dinner before you arrive?
        Yes, I will have dinner eaten before I arrive.
(neg)   *No, I will not (won't) have eaten before I arrive.*

Make sentences:

Example: *Will they have spoken before we leave?*
          Yes, they will have spoken before we leave.

1. Will he _____ finished his homework when the party starts? No, he _____ _____ _____ finished his homework.

2. What will you _____ remembered? I _____ _____ remembered all of the good times.

Words to use with Future Perfect:

by the time-

> *Chris will have finished the race **by the time** we arrive.*

when-

> *You will have spoken to Bill **when** she arrives.*

Make sentences:

Example: *We will have forgotten by the time we are 50 years old.*

1. Tony will have eaten desert _____   _____
_____ dinner is served.

2. She will have finished the milk _____ we wake up.

Perfect Continuous Tenses

Present Perfect Continuous

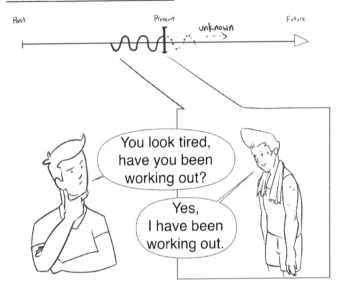

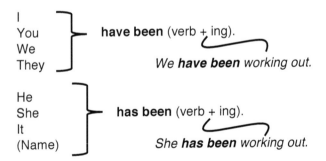

Make sentences:

Example: *Who has he been watching? He has been watching a Billy and John.*

1. Where has Steve _____ living? Steve _____ _____ living in Canada.

2. Why have _____ _____ studying? They _____ _____ studying because they have a test on Friday.

Present Perfect Continuous is used for:

actions that began in the past and continued to the present. Whether the action will continue into the future is unknown.

When have you been taking your medicine?
    I have been taking my medicine in the morning.

telling how long an action has been happening

How long have you been teaching?
    I have been teaching for seven years.

Words to use with Present Perfect Continuous:

for (amount of time)-
> *I have been working **for** 12 years.*

since (moment in time)-
> *Tom has been traveling **since** January.*

How long...?
> ***How long** have you been acting?*

Make sentences:

Example: *You have been reading for two hours.*

1. He has been studying _____ Monday.

2. _____   _____ have you been working here?

3. She has been talking _____ three hours.

Past Perfect Continuous

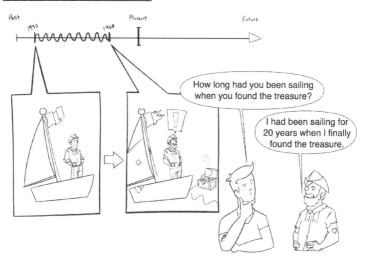

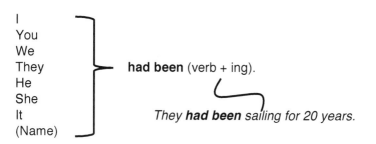

They **had been** sailing for 20 years.

Make sentences:

Example: *What had George been watching? George had been watching a scary movie.*

1. You were fat? What _____ you _____ eating. I had _____ _____ junk food for years.

Answer: had... been/been eating

Past Perfect Continuous is used for:

actions that were in progress when a Past Simple action happened

Had you been living in New York when you met Sam?
Yes, I had been living in New York when I met Sam.
(neg) *No, I had not (hadn't) been living in New York when I met Sam.*

Words to use with Past Perfect Continuous:

for (amount of time) –
*He had been trying **for 23 years when** he found the answer.*

since (moment in time) -
*It had been raining **since mid-May**.*

Make sentences:

Example: *She had been singing for 25 years when she won a Grammy.*

1. Steve had been waiting _____ 2011.

2. I had been working _____ two days.

Answers: 1. since 2. for

Future Perfect Continuous

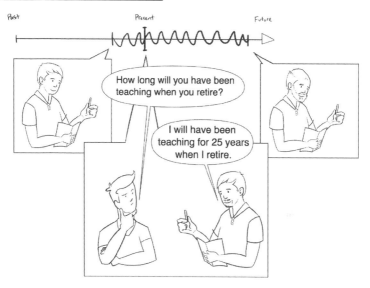

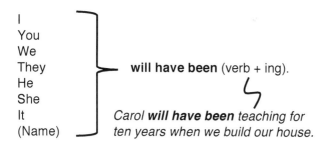

I	
You	
We	
They	**will have been** (verb + ing).
He	
She	
It	*Carol **will have been** teaching for*
(Name)	*ten years when we build our house.*

*A modal verb can replace *"will"* (makes tense Present
Perfect Continuous.) More is on page 45.

Make sentences:

Example: *It will have been downloading for five hours when the download completes.*

1. How long _____ we _____ _____ learning when we apply for college? We will _____ _____ learning for 16 years when we apply for college.

2. Our family _____ have _____ watching Christmas movies for two weeks by the time Christmas arrives.

Future Perfect Continuous is used for:

future actions that will be in progress when another foreseen future action happens

He will have been working at the bank for 25 years when he retires next month.

She will have been notified when her client arrives tomorrow.

They will have been sleeping for 14 hours when they wake up.

Answers: 1. will...have been/have been 2. will...been

Words to use with Future Perfect Continuous:

when-

> *Our children will have been going to school for 20 years **when** they finally start their careers.*

Make sentences:

Example: *You will have read 54 pages when you finish this book.*

1. How many pages will you have read _____ you finish this book? I will have read 54 pages _____ I finish this book.

How to use modal verbs:

Future Simple (possible modal verbs)

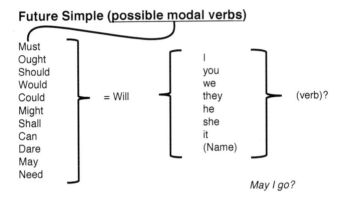

Must
Ought
Should
Would
Could   = Will
Might
Shall
Can
Dare
May
Need

I
you
we
they
he
she
it
(Name)

(verb)?

May I go?

Future Continuous (possible modal verbs)

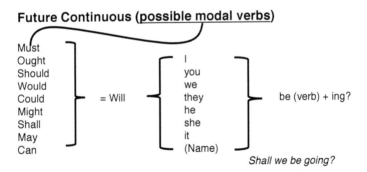

Must
Ought
Should
Would
Could   = Will
Might
Shall
May
Can

I
you
we
they
he
she
it
(Name)

be (verb) + ing?

Shall we be going?

Substitution of a modal verb for 'Will' in Future Continuous allows tense to be in Present Continuous also. *Should we be arguing?*

Future Perfect Continuous (<u>possible modal verbs</u>)

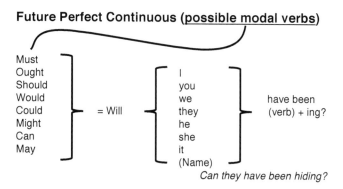

| Must Ought Should Would Could Might Can May | = Will | I you we they he she it (Name) | have been (verb) + ing? |

Can they have been hiding?

Substitution of a modal verb for 'Will' in Future Perfect Continuous makes the tense Present Perfect Continuous.   *Could we have been sleeping?*

Future Perfect (<u>possible modal verbs</u>)

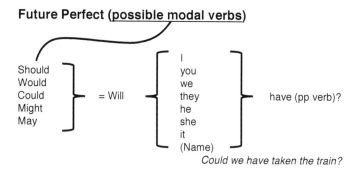

| Should Would Could Might May | = Will | I you we they he she it (Name) | have (pp verb)? |

Could we have taken the train?

Substitution of a modal verb for 'Will' in Future Perfect makes the tense Present Perfect.   *Should we have eaten the whole chicken?*

"will" is like "going to"

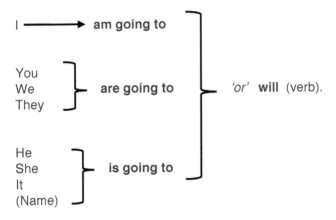

I ——————> am going to

You
We   are going to   'or' will (verb).
They

He
She   is going to
It
(Name)

I **am going to** try the spicy vegetables.
'or' I **will** try the spicy vegetables.

Differences between "will" and "going to"

"will" is used for:

deciding a future action at the *moment* you do it
I will have the spaghetti and meatballs.

promises
I promise I will take care of you.

making an offer
I'll give $4,500 for the car.

when asking "will…?"
Will you come?

"going to" is used for:

something scheduled that you're looking forward to
I'm going to fly to Spain!

deciding future actions or goals long before you do it
I'm going to publish a book.

making a prediction based on evidence
That car is going too fast. It's going to crash.

58 Common Verbs:

Many students can guess the correct pp verb after learning the verb. You might be surprised!

verb	past verb	pp verb
like	liked	liked
want	wanted	wanted
need	needed	needed

verb	past verb (irregular)	pp verb
be	was/were	been
become	became	become
begin	began	begun
bring	brought	brought
build	built	built
burn	burnt	burnt
buy	bought	bought
catch	caught	caught
choose	chose	chosen
come	came	come
cut	cut	cut
do	did	done
draw	drew	drawn
drink	drank	drunk
drive	drove	driven
eat	ate	eaten
fall	fell	fallen
feel	felt	felt
find	found	found
fly	flew	flown
forget	forgot	forgotten
get	got	gotten
give	gave	given
go	went	gone
have	had	had
hear	heard	heard

verb	past verb (irregular)	pp verb
know	knew	known
lay	laid	laid
leave	left	left
let	let	let
make	made	made
meet	met	met
pay	paid	paid
put	put	put
read	read	read
ride	rode	ridden
run	ran	run
say	said	said
see	saw	seen
sell	sold	sold
set	set	set
shut	shut	shut
sing	sang	sung
sit	sat	sat
sleep	slept	slept
speak	spoke	spoken
swim	swam	swum
take	took	taken
teach	taught	taught
think	thought	thought
understand	understood	understood
wake	woke	woken
wear	wore	worn
win	won	won
write	wrote	written

Long timeline exercise (next page):

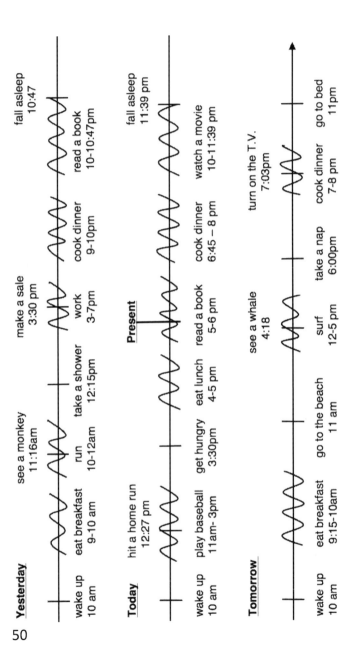

Yesterday

wake up
10 am

eat breakfast
9-10 am

see a monkey
11:16am

run
10-12am

take a shower
12:15pm

make a sale
3:30 pm

work
3-7pm

cook dinner
9-10pm

fall asleep
10:47

read a book
10-10:47pm

Today

hit a home run
12:27 pm

wake up
10 am

play baseball
11am- 3pm

get hungry
3:30pm

eat lunch
4-5 pm

Present

read a book
5-6 pm

cook dinner
6:45 – 8 pm

fall asleep
11:39 pm

watch a movie
10-11:39 pm

Tomorrow

wake up
10 am

eat breakfast
9:15-10am

go to the beach
11 am

see a whale
4:18

surf
12-5 pm

take a nap
6:00pm

turn on the T.V.
7:03pm

cook dinner
7-8 pm

go to bed
11pm

Practice Conversation

Present Simple:	Do you cook dinner? Yes, I cook every night.		Present Perfect:	Have you ever seen a monkey? Yes, I have seen a monkey.
Past Simple:	When did you wake up today? I woke up at 10:00 am.		Past Perfect:	Why were you so excited yesterday? I had seen a monkey.
Future Simple:	Will you go to the beach tomorrow? Yes, I will go to the beach.		Future Perfect:	Will you be hungry when you go to the beach tomorrow? No, I will have eaten breakfast.
Present Continuous:	What are you reading right now? I am reading a book on tenses.		Present Perfect Continuous:	What time have you been waking up lately? I have been waking up at 10:00 am.
Past Continuous:	What were you doing yesterday at 9:30am? I was eating breakfast.		Past Perfect Continuous:	Why did you take a shower at 12:15 yesterday? I had been running for two hours.
Future Continuous:	What will you be doing at 3:00 pm tomorrow? I will be surfing.		Future Perfect Continuous:	Why will you take a nap tomorrow at 6:00 pm? I will have been surfing for five hours.

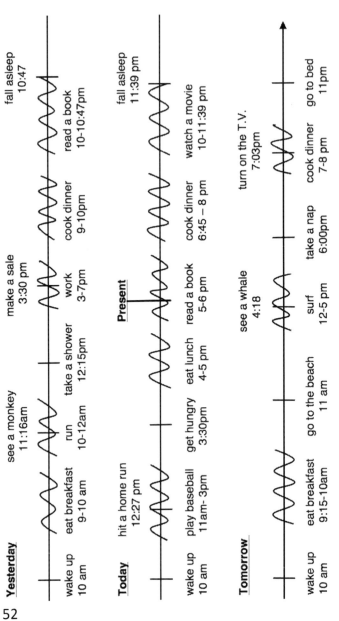

Yesterday

wake up
10 am

eat breakfast
9-10 am

see a monkey
11:16am

run
10-12am

take a shower
12:15pm

make a sale
3:30 pm

work
3-7pm

cook dinner
9-10pm

fall asleep
10:47

read a book
10-10:47pm

Today

hit a home run
12:27 pm

wake up
10 am

play baseball
11am- 3pm

get hungry
3:30pm

eat lunch
4-5 pm

Present

read a book
5-6 pm

cook dinner
6:45 – 8 pm

fall asleep
11:39 pm

watch a movie
10-11:39 pm

Tomorrow

wake up
10 am

eat breakfast
9:15-10am

go to the beach
11 am

see a whale
4:18

surf
12-5 pm

take a nap
6:00pm

turn on the T.V.
7:03pm

cook dinner
7-8 pm

go to bed
11pm

Practice Conversation:

Present Simple:	Do you cook dinner? Yes, _____ _____ every night.	Present Perfect:	Have you ever seen a monkey? Yes, I _____ _____ a monkey.
Past Simple:	When did you wake up today? I _____ _____ at 10:00 am.	Past Perfect:	Why were you so excited yesterday? I _____ _____ a monkey.
Future Simple:	Will you go to the beach tomorrow? Yes, _____ _____ go to the beach.	Future Perfect:	Will you be hungry when you go to the beach tomorrow? No, I _____ _____ breakfast.
Present Continuous:	What are you reading right now? I _____ _____ a book on tenses.	Present Perfect Continuous:	What time have you been waking up lately? I _____ _____ up at 10:00 am.
Past Continuous:	What were you doing yesterday at 9:30am? I _____ _____ breakfast.	Past Perfect Continuous:	Why did you take a shower at 12:15 yesterday? I _____ _____ for two hours.
Future Continuous:	What will you be doing at 3:00 pm tomorrow? I _____ _____ surfing.	Future Perfect Continuous:	Why will you take a nap tomorrow at 6:00 pm? I _____ _____ for five hours.

Mix Tenses:

Past Continuous and
Past Simple:

What were you doing when you saw a monkey?
I was running when I saw a monkey.

Past Simple and
Past Perfect Continuous:

Why did you take a shower?
I took a shower because I had been running.

Future Simple and
Future Perfect Continuous:

Why will you take a nap tomorrow?
I will take a nap because I will have been surfing for five
hours.

Future Continuous and
Present Simple:

What will you be doing when you see a whale?
I will be surfing when I see a whale.

Future Simple and
Present Continuous:

What will you do while you are cooking tomorrow?
I will turn on the TV while I am cooking tomorrow.

I hope this book has taught you a lot. Keep practicing, and thank you!

— Tyler Garrison

54

Notes: